Once upon a time, there were three little pigs who lived with their mummy in a big stone house.

One day, Mummy Pig said, "Children, it's time for you to go out and find your fortune in the big wide world." So she packed a little bag of food and a drink for each of them, and sent them on their way.

"Goodbye!" she called, as the three little pigs set off on their adventure. "Good luck, my dears, and remember to watch out for the big, bad wolf!"

"We will, Mummy," called the little pigs as they waved goodbye.

After a while, the three little pigs stopped for a rest and decided that they should each build a house to live in. Just then, they saw a farmer coming along the road with a wagon full of golden straw.

"Please, sir," said the first little pig, "may I have some of your straw to build myself a house?"

"Yes, little pig," said the farmer, "of course you can."

So the first little pig built his house of straw. Soon it was finished. It looked very good indeed, and the first little pig was happy.

The other two little pigs set off on their journey together and, after a while, they met a man carrying a large bundle of sticks.

"Please, sir," said the second little pig, "may I have some of your sticks to build myself a house?"

"Yes, little pig," said the man, "of course you can."

So the second little pig built his house of sticks. Soon it was finished. It looked very good indeed, and the second little pig was happy.

The third little pig set off on his journey alone. He saw lots of people with wagons of straw and bundles of sticks, but he did not stop until he met a man with a cart filled to the brim with bricks.

"Please, sir," said the third little pig, "may I have some bricks to build myself a house?"

"Yes, little pig," said the man, "of course you can."

So the third little pig built his house of bricks. Soon it was finished. It looked very good indeed. It was strong and solid, and the third little pig was very, very pleased.

That evening, the big, bad wolf was walking along the road. He was very hungry and looking for something good to eat. He saw the first little pig's house of straw and looked in through the window.

"Yum, yum," he said to himself, licking his lips. "This little pig would make a most tasty dinner."

So in his friendliest voice, the wolf called through the window, "Little pig, little pig, please let me in!"

But the first little pig remembered his Mummy's warning, so he replied, "No, no, I won't let you in, not by the hair on my chinny-chin-chin!"

This made the wolf really angry. "Very well!" he roared. "I'll huff and I'll puff, and I'll blow your house down!"

The poor little pig was very afraid, but he still would not let the wolf in. So the wolf huffed... and he puffed... and he BLEW the straw house down.

Then the big, bad wolf chased the little pig and – gobbled him up!

But the wolf was still hungry! He walked down the road and soon came to the house made of sticks. He looked through the window and called to the second little pig, "Little pig, little pig, please let me in."

"No, no!" cried the second little pig. "I won't let you in, not by the hair on my chinny-chin-chin!"

"Very well," cried the wolf. "Then I'll huff and I'll puff, and I'll blow your house down!"

And that's just what the big, bad wolf did. He huffed… and he puffed… and he BLEW the stick house down! Then he gobbled up the second little pig.

But the big, bad wolf was still hungry. So he walked down the road and soon came to the house made of bricks. He looked through the window and called to the third little pig, "Little pig, little pig, please let me in."

"No, no!" cried the third little pig. "I won't let you in, not by the hair on my chinny-chin-chin!"

"Very well," roared the big, bad wolf. "I'll huff and I'll puff, and I'll blow your house down!"

So the wolf huffed and he puffed… he HUFFED and he PUFFED… and he HUFFED and he PUFFED some more, but he could not blow the brick house down!

By now the big, bad wolf was very, very angry. He scrambled up onto the roof and began to climb down through the chimney.

But the third little pig was a clever little pig, and he had put a big pot of boiling water to bubble on the fire.

When the wolf came down the chimney, he landed – ker-splosh! – right in the middle of the pot of boiling water! He burned his bottom so badly that he ran out of the house and down the road as fast as his legs could carry him, and was never heard of again!

The third little pig was very pleased
with his house of bricks and lived in it
for many years, happy and content.
And nothing was heard of the big,
bad wolf ever again.